D1383821

Words to Know Before You Read

bed

chair

giggles

grass

hear

outside

purrs

sink

www.rourkepublishing.com

Edited by Luana Mitten
Illustrated by Anita DuFalla
Art Direction and Page Layout by Renee Brady

Library of Congress Cataloging-in-Publication Data

Cleland, Jo
 Kitty Come Down! / Jo Cleland.
     p. cm. -- (Little Birdie Books)
 Includes bibliographical references and index.
 ISBN 978-1-61741-808-2(hard cover) (alk. paper)
 ISBN 978-1-61236-012-6 (soft cover)
 Library of Congress Control Number: 2011924660

Rourke Publishing
Printed in the United States of America, North Mankato, Minnesota
060711
060711CL

www.rourkepublishing.com - rourke@rourkepublishing.com
Post Office Box 643328 Vero Beach, Florida 32964

Kitty Come Down!

By Jo Cleland

Illustrated by Anita DuFalla

Where is Kitty?

Look under the bed.

9

Look under the sink.

Still Kitty does not come. 11

Shh! I hear Kitty.

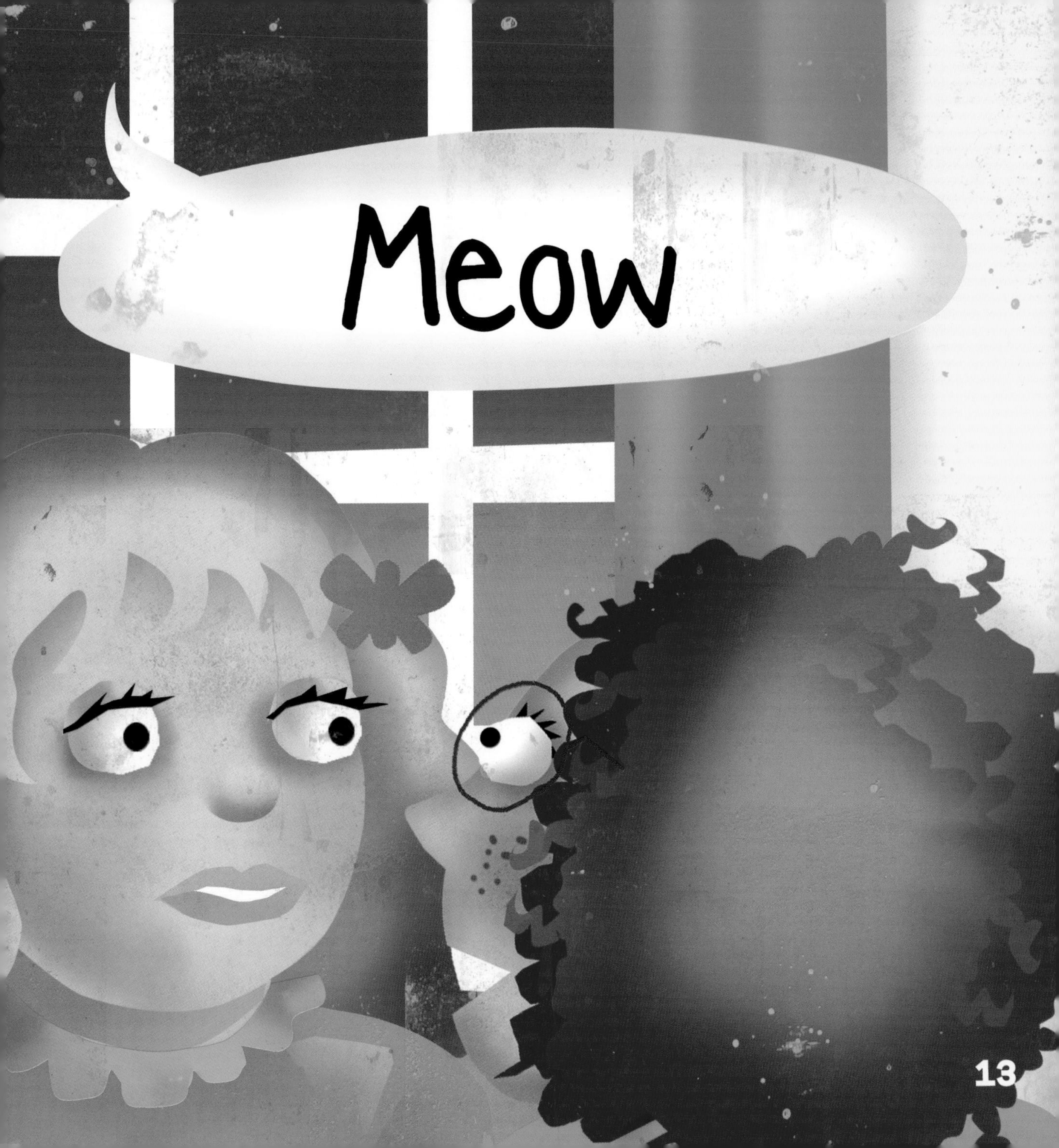
Meow

Look in the tree.

14

16

Kitty, come down!

21

After Reading Activities

You and the Story...

Where did the kids look for Kitty?

Where did they find Kitty?

Why do you think cats like to hide?

Think about your favorite animal. What is something that your favorite animals like to do?

Words You Know Now...

Rhyme Time – Write the words on a piece of paper and then write a word that rhymes with each word.

bed	hear
chair	outside
giggles	purrs
grass	sink

You Could...Write About Your Favorite Animal

- Decide what your favorite animal is.

- Think about what you want to write about your favorite animal.

- Choose what kind of paper you want to use to write your story.
    - plain paper
    - colored paper
    - lined paper
    - blank storybook

- Decide how you want to start your story.

- Be sure to include details about your characters in your story.

- Draw pictures to illustrate your story.

- Get creative!

About the Author

Jo Cleland enjoys writing books, composing songs, and making games. When she was a girl she loved to feed the cats on the farm.

About the Illustrator

Acclaimed for its versatility in style, Anita DuFalla's work has appeared in many educational books, newspaper articles, and business advertisements and on numerous posters, book and magazine covers, and even giftwraps. Anita's passion for pattern is evident in both her artwork and her collection of 400 patterned tights. She lives in the Friendship neighborhood of Pittsburgh, Pennsylvania with her son, Lucas.